10708209

Written, Edited, Formatted, Designed by Triffawna Witt.

Cover illustration design using Canva by Triffawna Witt.

Self-published by the author and fulfilled through various platforms.

ISBN:

979-8-9899211-8-8

Where to keep reading more to fill the negative space
and get lost between the lines, please follow:

Website:

http://letsgetlostbetweenthelines.com

Instagram:

@letsgetlostbetweenthelines

Email:

letsgetlostbetweenthelines@gmail.com

PO BOX:

Triffawna Witt

PO BOX 872468

Wasilla, AK, 99687

you're why the book can't be shut

Books by Author:

you're why the book can't be shut

2

While its only one book on this page like a good poem you can't simply continue reading without a line prior to the second. Follow my journey as a budding author.

Triffawna Witt

you're why
the book
can't be shut:

Collection of Love Poems, Prose, Thoughts for
Heartbreak, Relationships, Trauma Healing

By:

Triffawna Witt

Thank you to all the **reasons** and **seasons** that have **occurred** in my life to be **my muse** even though the pages that follow are filled with things..**I didn't say.**

you're why the book can't be shut

Like a bad book I can't seem to put away
Each turn of the page it slices my finger tips
Ingesting every word my eyes do stay
The sweetest sour that could ever hit my lips
New chapters keep being started
Just holding the book open wide
At this point I am my own martyr
A fan of the dialogue and ride
Is it ink that's never ending or my blood
Holding the page longer it seals the cut
Get to the bottom just to be thrown back to mud
You're why the book can't just be shut

@letsgetlostbetweenthelines
©

you're why the book can't be shut

things need to go quiet

Words so many words I use to write

About this that whatever would keep me out of sight

At least typing helped me feel more in my shell

Or was it helping me to come out of that hell

Still unsure if in it or out of it is up or down

Much like a smile or frown is to a clown

A most basic analogy to help you understand

Sometimes things need to go quiet

For reason or another to take a long soloist riot

Even a crab grows weary and outgrown

Tired of huddling in the small dark and alone

Crawling through outside finding a new home

Refuge from all that had to be

Did it have to be, now I'm starting to see

@letsgetlostbetweenthelines

you're why the book can't be shut

we postpone our dreams

Tired of the world's endless cycle of dismay

Yearning for a day when hatred will fade away

Like a zombie, we wander through our routines

Silent voices cry, overshadowed by life's machines

Seeking a moment when joy will come and stay

We postpone our dreams, fearing they'll decay

But within one breath, one precious moment's chime

Our worth shall flourish, transcending mere dime

Awakening to love's embrace, for it is our prime

No longer bound by the shackles of time

We dance in the freedom, our spirits unchained

@letsgetlostbetweenthelines

©

you're why the book can't be shut

nervous butterflies

In the grocery store I glimpse your eyes,

Between the aisles, my heart takes flight,

Nervous butterflies flutter inside,

Wanting to say hello, lips sealed tight,

Across the crowded shelves, did our gazes meet?

But uncertainty lingers, for you're not free,

Yet in that stolen moment, wish you did see me

@letsgetlostbetweenthelines

©

you're why the book can't be shut

break bread

Divine intervention seeing same outcome

Wondering where God's coming from

What is the end game from here

When will it come into fruition and not fear

So many questions between the hidden moment

Why can't all the past shortcomings go dormant

Like trees in the fall losing their leaves

Time escaping faster then water in sieves

Awake asleep does it matter, the feeling is lost

Forever staying standing frozen frost

No, heaped over bending breaking

After every encounter and dream from afar, shaking

To do the reckless and stupid, is God playing cupid

See what I did there overthrowing and overthinking

Shrunk down into a tiny ship bound for sinking

Doesn't matter which way you spin the world

She keeps on spinning nice and swirled and twirled

If, like that word does a whole lot of good

If you would see me passing by where you stood

Break bread with your demons tell them ditto

Cause I need to say goodbye to that kiddo

@letsgetlostbetweenthelines

you're why the book can't be shut

<u>*steal me*</u>

Can you feel the pull

Pulling of gravity towards you

Indescribable feeling it is

To stand here still is impossible

With these lips of mine

Can you see it

The sugar still lingers from you

Come back here to me

Claim all that's yours

Wishing upon a star

Like night steals the day

We'll be gone from this world

Faster than a comet

Flying through the clouds

Just you and me

Above everybody else

Cause nobody we'll need

@letsgetlostbetweenthelines

©

you're why the book can't be shut

<u>bottom of these bubbles</u>

Maybe I will just fill the tub with bubbles

Lay in it till my fingers turn to wrinkles

Cause that is the best way to waste time

At least it will be relaxing

Or maybe I will go out like you are

When the sun starts to rise

And alcohol fills my veins

I will call you up just to hear your voice

Maybe if I lay here long enough

I will find you at the bottom of these bubbles

Pulling me down deep in love once again

@letsgetlostbetweenthelines

©

you're why the book can't be shut

drowning at night

Late at night is the most peaceful time,
the world seems to shut off
I hide myself away in these moments,
away from universe and problems
Locked away in my room,
laying my head down to rest
And close my eyes,
away from the light
Pulling the blankets over my head,
suddenly it is there I'm not alone
Words begin to talk from all around,
voices bouncing inside my mind
My own voice that remains alive,
neglected thoughts of the day
Things I would've thought, said, or did,
one thing stays
Is thoughts of you,
I cannot escape you no matter what I try

you're why the book can't be shut

(Cont.) drowning at night

It seems the harder I try to forget,

thoughts of you creep back inside

Little ants at work they creep and crawl around,

busy and moving

Appears forevermore,

thoughts of you beaten my brain into submission

My body seems to be numb all around,

time slowly creeps by

Tossing turning in these sheets,

drowning at night will be my undoing

It's become apparent,

I'm curse to a life of no sleep

Cause once again hiding away does nothing,

when you leave me here

With thoughts of you

@letsgetlostbetweenthelines

©

you're why the book can't be shut

tears pour

We can be strangers, run away in the night

Never to turn back no regrets

What is life without risks

What is life without pain

Love just reminds us why

That is how we know it is real, right

When the tears pour into my hands

And fill your ears with my pleas

Then again why is love so hurtful

We fight just to turn around and makeup

That makeup love sure is the best

I know to never have felt this

Maybe I am just selfish

Sometimes I feel stupid but

After all, you have loved me once before

@letsgetlostbetweenthelines

©

you're why the book can't be shut

sometimes

If you love a flower don't pick it up
It dies and ceases to be what you love
So, if you love a flower, let it be
The good thing is not about possession
Love is about appreciation
Sometimes, the flower picks you

@letsgetlostbetweenthelines

you're why the book can't be shut

that night after the dare

The mountain is high and the valley is wide

Like some unspoken law I chose to abide

When the moment arises resorting a good hide

To say we laughed would have to say I lied

No exchanges take place beyond here

Swirls of butterflies and exasperated fear

God surely placed us in time so near

Past stuck in present can kick ya in the rear

It's one foot in front of the other

To be behind myself and surely shove her

Say hey stupid go get your lover

Instead I duck duck goose and take cover

That means to chicken out

Walk away no run away drive and reroute

Sit at home in my room to pout

Wondering when the next tile will need grout

Bricks in this pathway to nowhere

Golden shimmering hopeful what is always there

The next turn the next aisle the next stop is rare

It all ended that night after the dare

@letsgetlostbetweenthelines

©

you're why the book can't be shut

you're a standing deer

The jagged pain in my side

Reminds me to grip my mind

Its like the new fair ride

That just isn't your kind

Be the best time

But leaves you the guilt of a crime

Laughing with a friend

But gone somewhere else

Now in a nightmare that will never end

You're a standing deer

Stuck in the headlights

Feeling the tears

Want to move, but can't

People shout through your ears

You become your biggest fear

@letsgetlostbetweenthelines

©

you're why the book can't be shut

<u>my daydream of you</u>

Telling myself I have met you once upon a dream

Things like this could not possibly happen

I wonder what I could have done to deserve this

Your kisses so sweet, wanting more

Not able to think, not able to speak

Silenced by their touch upon my lips

Frozen forever in time with every touch

You could suffocate me with your poison

And I would be completely satisfied

My mind high, clouded by the thoughts of you

Over and over again they consume my body

I do not mind it at all that you are there

Because even when you're not here

My daydream of you is just as lovely

@letsgetlostbetweenthelines

you're why the book can't be shut

<u>complicate</u>

It was really quite simple
Find who makes you happy
And choose them everyday
What could we possibly complicate

@letsgetlostbetweenthelines
©

you're why the book can't be shut

<u>*"I'm fine"*</u>

All that I touch withers and disappears
It seems that the roles have been switched
That which is here is just all of my fears
Left out in the cold, alone and ditched

Once alive and well with sunshine
Now bitten and covered with the cold
Smiles and lies to play off "I'm fine"
But really frowns and tears is what is told

Taught from birth that all endings are happy
Believing in all those fairytales
But in reality they're all sad and sappy
I rather be pierced in the heart by a nail
Then continue to live life a lie

@letsgetlostbetweenthelines
©

you're why the book can't be shut

<u>ignorant, happy, dumb</u>

Praise be the one who quit

Slow burns wicked end of the flame

Chaos and pain moment it was lit

Three cheers for the winner and tame

Where is the support to rebuild the house

Even outreach that's there, is sad

Told to sit still for the spouse

Things should be better, that'd be rad

Let go let God I am told over

Tired of being tired and numb

The world now feels nowhere near sober

I remember being ignorant, happy, dumb

No one to overjoy the keeper of fire

@letsgetlostbetweenthelines

you're why the book can't be shut

too much the same

Fairytales fuck your fairytale and all their lies
Fluttery sugar-coated amber glassed I despise
No one told me how unrealistic of the end game
From let down your hair to what's in a name

All knowing no man is climbing any tower
They're not buying or picking the sweetest flower
Dinners aren't being planned and devoured
Why have I always been surrounded by a coward

Usually three strikes and you're out
Who assigned me the play past ball four route
Options one through four all treated me poor
Should've could've showed them all the door

you're why the book can't be shut

(Cont.) too much the same

Is it just written to be unwritten all men suck

Do all women really feel this shitty and stuck

Not all the time is so cloudy and dark

There's lots of good moments that make their mark

Devil is strong when you're in the sea

Praying daily the storm surely leaves me be

Fairytales and the sea are too much the same

Predictability of getting drowned are in the name

@letsgetlostbetweenthelines

©

you're why the book can't be shut

<u>can't go a day</u>

Believe what I say
It's feeling is bliss
I can't go a day

A day without

Will surely kill me
Now do not doubt
Just wait and see

I will have it soon
In my arms once more
We will lay under the moon
With the stars we will soar

Our own world tonight
Held close to my heart
This love is out of sight
Never seen far apart
Captured forever in this place

@letsgetlostbetweenthelines

you're why the book can't be shut

<u>*horse blinders*</u>

It makes sense now that the darkness is out

Wouldn't call it light is on since the deed is so bad

Horse blinders over rose glasses got me through the days

What do you wear where you're forced to remove them

@letsgetlostbetweenthelines

©

you're why the book can't be shut

awake in a world that refuses to live sober

To be in this world numb and complacent

Concerned brows and bitch face lives free rent

Having no issues voicing my opinion

Speak words and feelings would cut like an onion

Letting them fly out bees defending their hive

Sticking up for myself man to feel that alive

Too bad my mouth remains to be shut

Conflicts left to fester and twist holes in my gut

Feel awake in a world that refuses to live sober

Even after all those seasons never have felt broker

@letsgetlostbetweenthelines

©

you're why the book can't be shut

<u>fun and pies</u>

Every boyfriend official and not have cheated
Why do so many words easily rhyme with cheated
Treated repeated defeated heated deleted conceited
Needed preceded proceeded exceeded pleaded
So many words to encompass the act
Like all males have bonded together made a pact
The homewreckers aren't trustworthy either
Such a small world nowhere to hide neither
The time you take to scroll at a red light
Is longer then it takes you to save someone's night
Everyone is out for themselves out here
A friend of a friend won't even crack from fear
Or not telling makes enemy of my enemy a friend
So why doesn't no one ever break or bend
Stand up against all the enabling and lies
Afraid they'll miss out on the fun and pies
There's only been one person to tell me straight
Utmost respect for that girl even if I realized it too late.

@letsgetlostbetweenthelines

©

you're why the book can't be shut

goes up

What goes up

Must come down

In that case

You'll come around

@letsgetlostbetweenthelines

©

you're why the book can't be shut

<u>holding hands with a memory</u>

And there you are
Back again after last season
Swore it wouldn't be too far
Coming back with such reason
As if winter could forget summer

It's long and lonely demise
Why would you tell me of a change
Haven't spoken in years no surprise
Ghosts to each other so strange
Left again holding hands with a memory

But never truly grasping reality
A haunting reminder of what used to be
In the echoes of our love's cemetery
And somehow still holds a grip on me
Our love, frozen in time, ready to thaw

@letsgetlostbetweenthelines

©

you're why the book can't be shut

gateway

Love is a gateway to adventures. Such glorious of a gateway
should definitely be opened. This wonderful feeling moment
is a necessity that every human being needs to experience.
Love is a reality and fantasy intertwined and interchangeable.

We are the gatekeepers.

@letsgetlostbetweenthelines

©

you're why the book can't be shut

<u>*under this big dipper*</u>

I want to be held by you

Act like I got nowhere else to be

Because that is true, I have no other plans

So just come on lay down over here

Wrap your strong arms around me

We will stare at the stars all night long

And when the night air gets too cold

Hiding under this blanket we'll be

Stars high above us we will get lost

Lips pressing together as one

Eyes staring back at each other

Hands tracing all the curves

Bodies tangled all up together

Just you and me under this big dipper

Forever, till the sun comes back up again

@letsgetlostbetweenthelines

©

you're why the book can't be shut

can winter forget

In the depths of winter's embrace
Once again, you grace my space
Promising a renewal, a chance to mend
Yet, I find myself unsure, afraid to pretend
Can winter forget the touch of the sun

With each passing day, the distance is clear
Years have gone by, leaving echoes to adhere
Like specters we roam this desolate plain
Lost souls intertwined, forever in pain
Embracing memories, unable to let go

@letsgetlostbetweenthelines
©

you're why the book can't be shut

(Cont.) can winter forget

62

But reality's grasp eludes our grasp

A bittersweet reminder, a moment's gasp

In the graveyard of love, echoes remain

Whispering secrets, dancing in the rain

Our love, frozen and forever set free

Embrace the present, create love anew

For winter's frost cannot erase what's true

Let us break free from this haunting tether

And in the thaw, a chance for love to bloom

Though time may freeze us, we're not bound

For love's flame, in embers, can still be found

@letsgetlostbetweenthelines

©

you're why the book can't be shut

<u>*ungrateful you are*</u>

Getting a better look
At what you already knew
Something that you took
You picked from very few
But yet still wanted more
Ungrateful you are
Winter knocks summers door

@letsgetlostbetweenthelines

©

you're why the book can't be shut

no one else

He's like the deep south

The place where I'm from

Lips so sweet on my mouth

Rich and juicy as the red plum

Eyes so blue no sky could compare

Caring and courageous they always shine

No one else is as fair

And he's always going to be mine

@letsgetlostbetweenthelines

©

you're why the book can't be shut

<u>you owned the place</u>

I still remember the day I met you

Walked in like you owned the place

From the shadow emerged with that smirk

Seen you sipping on your whiskey

Caught me staring at you

I was lost deep in your hazel eyes

Your charming smile made my head spin

Words were like a sweet lullaby to my ears

Cowboy casanova you were drawing me in closer

@letsgetlostbetweenthelines

©

you're why the book can't be shut

rambling

It all fell into place from there

I sat down next to you and you started talking

Rambling on about your whiskey

Rambling on how I must've been the prettiest girl

Rambling on and on but I wasn't listening

I couldn't believe that love at first sight was real

Before I knew it you asked for a kiss

@letsgetlostbetweenthelines

©

you're why the book can't be shut

<u>I was your prey</u>

Just a kiss on the cheek, you said
Really deep down I wanted more
End of the night I found myself without
You tracked me down like I was your prey
Before long we were talking again
Before long we shared our first kiss
Before long we did more than we could handle

@letsgetlostbetweenthelines
©

you're why the book can't be shut

<u>*go back to that summer*</u>

Like any other ordinary love story

We fell in and out of love

Life consumed us and we fell apart

Too fast the time flew by

Wish I could go back to that summer

Where all those sweet memories of you are

I can't look at a truck without thoughts of you

I can't go back to that place without seeing you

@letsgetlostbetweenthelines

©

you're why the book can't be shut

<u>every now and then</u>

The day I laid my eyes on you

That was the day I would never forget

Every now and then something reminds me

Now every time I hear a pretty bird

I wish it was my phone receiving a text

And I think back to every time I smiled

It was because of you

It was your whiskey memory that started it all

@letsgetlostbetweenthelines

©

you're why the book can't be shut

dust spot

I don't know who needs to hear this today

But you can't expect

The person who broke you

To piece you back together

You can't expect them to mend you

To mold you back to the place you were

That place is gone

That person is dead

That dust spot on the shelf

Is so different

Shattered

Broken

Smeared

Yet you stay

Waiting for the hot glue

And the sticky tack to adhere

Stuck onto each fiber and crack of you

Shards between splinters throughout

@letsgetlostbetweenthelines

©

you're why the book can't be shut

<u>*in the bustling aisles*</u>

In the bustling aisles, our gazes entwined,

Heartbeats quicken, passions unbind,

Whispered yearnings ignite, secrets unwind,

Silent words dance, emotions aligned,

In a crowded realm, a fleeting decree,

Fate entwined us, as you glanced back at me,

In that stolen moment, souls found sanctuary

@letsgetlostbetweenthelines

©

you're why the book can't be shut

sea of dreams

A giant blackhole is where all my thoughts go sometimes

Is this where my first memory of you has fallen

Did it grow a mind of its own and get lost somehow

Is it lost between a dream and reality

Or was it really that important

It must have had some greatness

If not, then in reality you should be here now

How could one have a relationship with a stranger

I must have met you once before in a dream somewhere

Do things this amazing really just appear to someone

Like an apple which has fallen out of a tree

It seems that you have fallen to me from heaven

Cheesy but it must have hurt falling down to earth

Or is it really earth at all anymore where I reside

How can one be so sure of the surroundings

To say one thing is something and another is another thing

This must not be earth at all anymore then

Cause a person this amazing cannot be so real

you're why the book can't be shut

(Cont.) sea of dreams

Lots of questions race through my mind

And run down inside my arm

Selfishly they spark out along my fingers

So carefully picked they pour out of this pen

They are spread viciously along this paper

To be read by hungry eyes and jealous minds

So is this a reality after all that everyone inhabits

Or is this whole thing we call life just one big dream

No that is not quite right at all

It must be illegal to seem this perfect so early

But maybe everybody is simply dream within a dream

If you are living your own dream and I'm living mine

Then this is crime we are both taking part in

The final question seems to be slowly revealing itself

Whose reality are we truly living in this giant sea of dreams

@letsgetlostbetweenthelines

©

you're why the book can't be shut

shattering glass

A cruel world is where I dwell

Poisoned with greed and hate

I too fell under the spell

Now all in blood I'm left to fate

I was not always like this

A beauty beyond compare

The devil is who stole a kiss

Which is not all that fair

It's quarter till midnight

Still laying on the bathroom floor

Thinking about turning on the light

But it's too close to the door

If I move somebody might hear

The shattering glass within me

Draws out more than just a tear

Sharp remains is all I will be

It's so hard to breath with this pain

Each one feels like my last

Like I will be left to die in vain

If so I hope it happens fast

you're why the book can't be shut

<u>open your eyes</u>

After all that's said and done

Its quality is different sometimes

But no matter about the sun

Will always rise and fall once again

A new day will occur

Your troubles will wash away

Second chances are in your favor

Now is your time, today, right now

As you watch that sun rise

Don't forget to open your eyes

Open your eyes to possibilities

Dreams will become reality

Today is your day.

@letsgetlostbetweenthelines

©

you're why the book can't be shut

never allowed

Sure, but what about feeling it immensely for years
every day every second it's on your mind so loud that
you were never allowed to feel it really. Everything and
everyone around you kept moving on. Now time has
gone by that you still think it was yesterday even though
you can't remember it and remember everything about it
all at once because you've lived it every second since it
happened. So numbing that it's so unreal to have even
happened as if it's from someone else's book.

@letsgetlostbetweenthelines

you're why the book can't be shut

moon phase

Wrong time

Wrong day

Wrong year

Right place

Right look

Right feeling

Blame the high power

Universe is at fault

Moon phase out of whack

Planets are all fighting

We're waiting for the stars to align

To take the time wasted back

To go back to the day we met

To make that our special year

It was all over the place

Can't it be all over with that look

You sure left me good with those feelings

@letsgetlostbetweenthelines

©

92

you're why the book can't be shut

<u>*on accident*</u>

Why now

Why now in this moment

Why now after all this time

Isn't that just so classic

If history is to repeat itself

But nothing happens on accident

Tell me what to expect

To expect from you this time

@letsgetlostbetweenthelines

©

you're why the book can't be shut

of adolescent youth

I wasn't prepared

No one prepared me

God didn't send a warning sign

Just like that falling star

Back to the earth

Whoosh, gone

Let me go back to that

Passing comet

Say something worthwhile

Our first meeting

First hellos first looks

What would be different

Met you in the chaos

Of adolescent youth

Where we don't or can't

Fully understand and appreciate

What's handed to us

@letsgetlostbetweenthelines

you're why the book can't be shut

<u>*dear*</u>

I start this letter out to you

Making it permanent by using pen

First words I write are Dear Boo

Cause I picked you over all the men

You won me over with your charm

Since then you've owned my heart

Keeping me tied onto your arm

I truly loved you from the start

We will never be apart

@letsgetlostbetweenthelines

©

you're why the book can't be shut

<u>*keep us grounded*</u>

Our love is like a flicker of a flame

Strongest hot when we are together

But even a candle burns away

Just a gust of air comes around

Extinguishing our love

Don't let your guard down

Protect us from strong winds

Tie us down with your love

Keep us grounded

Stand and hold me tight

Let me know everything will be alright

@letsgetlostbetweenthelines

©

let it burn

Happy. A million definitions. Only one true outcome. It's what everyone is dying for. They say home of the free because of the brave. How many of us are truly brave. Brave enough to go out and get what we want. Simply none of us are. We are all just sitting here waiting. Waiting for what we are use to. The world wound up and strung up so tight. The very string the globe is hanging on by a thread. Just one word and a specific word can change your whole outlook. It's how you choose to take those words. Our view gets clouded and misconceived. A fetus still growing we all are. Kicking and moving in this universe. Just screaming to get out and break free. So, you ask me what happiness is. I say its nothing and everything all at once. A strangers smile to a dogs wagging tail. Both innocent and overseen daily. Much like everyone today. Everyone searching for their happiness. Take it into your own hands. Stop and smile back or ask to pet that dog. You don't have to go out and dress up. Just to show up and take it off. They be shooting up and smoking down. Just to fly high and feel low. I rather be your happiness than your drug. Cause like every drug it only last for so long. And happiness is but a word made up. It is an endless road with only one outcome. Spend your whole life searching. Wasting. Ruining. When simply you should just let it be and live. Take hold of those little glimmers as the kids call it these days.

Hold that magnifying glass and let it burn.

@letsgetlostbetweenthelines

©

you're why the book can't be shut

in the dark

What happens in the dark, comes out in the light
Putting up a fight, trying to take flight
But in the end, surrendering to the night
Unburdening the soul, in shadows we unite
Finding solace in the darkness, where our demons ignite
Leaving behind the sun, embracing the moons sight
Embracing the moons sight, where secrets ignite
In its pale glow, we find our own respite
This is just silly right, bringing it all to light
Past feelings to anoint, what's the point

@letsgetlostbetweenthelines
©

you're why the book can't be shut

peace with your past

I went back to our place today
Walked up onto the rocks and sat
Right down on the edge
Walking up wasn't quite the same
I had butterflies in my stomach but
They weren't the same
These ones were toxic and painful
It seemed that each step I took
They squirmed more and more
As if they were eating their way out
To think they're more scared of this place
Scared more than I am is ironic
Maybe that's why I came back really
People are always saying you must make peace
Peace with your past to live for the future
But aren't we all living in the past
Many think you're the reason I came back

@letsgetlostbetweenthelines

you're why the book can't be shut

not nature's fault

Why on earth would someone come back

Back to the place where all their problems started

Then again what do places have to do with anything

For it is not nature's fault

As water which falls down mountains into rivers

It's only purpose is to cleanse the earth

Plain and simple, to take anything in its way

But like all things that fall they must get up

Water falls and goes through transformation

It returns to the heavens

So how I wish that were true

Sadly you will still find me sitting here

Sitting in the same spot

Lost all track of time and not longing to get up

In reality, that is the very reason I came here

To get up once again after you.

@letsgetlostbetweenthelines

©

you're why the book can't be shut

power over everything

Water

A natural flowing element that has no limitations

There's no stopping it once it has started

It has the power to destroy and heal again

Love

Love is like water

Power over everything

@letsgetlostbetweenthelines

you're why the book can't be shut

<u>carry me away</u>

Little rolls washing flatter and flatter

Up onto the sand

The longer I sit the closer the water creeps

As if they are trying to catch me

Wishing to carry me away and drown me

Into its embrace

Although drowning right now

Is the least of my worries

When you're still out there

@letsgetlostbetweenthelines

©

you're why the book can't be shut

safe and sound

With you I am not lost, I'm found

Once glance, I'm caught forever

Whenever I look, Deep into your eyes

I feel as though, At the beach

Staring into the horizon, Grounded and content

Blue like waters below, I'm engulfed in a trance

It feels like home to me, Safe and sound

Forever caught, Deep inside your love

@letsgetlostbetweenthelines

©

you're why the book can't be shut

<u>*frozen in time*</u>

I wish I could lay my eyes upon you

Staring right back at me, such dorky smile

You don't have to say a thing

That smile is cause of me, surely

Cause my smile is because of you

Right next to you my body lays

Arms pull me in closer

We just lie there looking at each other

Frozen in time without worry

No words needed because that look

Just one kiss will break our silence

Such precious moments to ruin

Stuck right here lost

@letsgetlostbetweenthelines
©

you're why the book can't be shut

they creep slowly

Looking around for something, a sign

Leaves cover the ground now

Crackling with each step further step

Into an unknown abyss

Hoping for something

Nothing

Searching for

Any evidence of life

Would be nice to receive

Glance over my shoulder

Being cautious of those feelings

For they creep slowly

Waiting and ready

Like lions they

Pounce

Kill

Devour me whole

@letsgetlostbetweenthelines

©

you're why the book can't be shut

breathe life back into this void

I've had my heart broken too many times

Trusted too much only to get nothing in return

Put walls up just to see who would climb over

Baby you came out of nowhere

And torn my walls down

I feel like myself again

Or was before the real me

What is existence now

Now that you're here

I don't want to lose you

Lose this feeling

Feelings, yikes

I've spent so long avoiding all of that

Teach me again how to live beyond existing

One kiss at a time

Breathe life back into this void

That I have drawn back into

@letsgetlostbetweenthelines

you're why the book can't be shut

<u>*gracious charm*</u>

She didn't need picked, but to enjoy

Admiring its dainty beauty from afar

To allow seeds to scatter and flourish

Years to come he walk by that meadow

And lay down in its caress and gracious charm

Sometimes I wonder what it would've felt like

To encompass that match thrown down within

A blazing rage spilled across my flowers

Growing back more beautiful then before

@letsgetlostbetweenthelines

©

you're why the book can't be shut

<u>tell me you'd love me so</u>

Would you go with me be alright

And hold my hand forever

Tell me you'd never leave my sight

When the sun goes down

Are you gonna hold onto me tight

Sing me a lullaby and kiss me

Cause you love me so even through the night

@letsgetlostbetweenthelines

©

you're why the book can't be shut

falling down

Alone way out here, But I can sense you are near

Reach out and touch me, You surely set me free

Just slow down and listen, Hear snowflakes glisten

Falling down to the ground, Freezing solid by the pound

Come sit down now, Let your mind think wow

Cause it is a blessing, Believe me I'm not guessing

That what we are, Will really go far

When it's all said and done, We are together having fun

They'll look at me and you, To think what we already knew

Like snowflakes long travel, We will never unravel.

@letsgetlostbetweenthelines

©

you're why the book can't be shut

must be a crime

Hold me close, Whisper something sweet

Kiss me on the nose, Listen to my heart beat

Grab my hand, Lead the way

We'll dance to the band, And forget the day

Don't be shy, Share your sweet smile

On the clouds we'll fly, Everyone will have to wait awhile

Cause this night is like no other, My whole life I've waited

I wouldn't want to share this with another, Together fated

In the middle of the floor, Twirling around like a top

Only makes me want more, Never want this night to stop

Outside to the stars he leads me, Moment lost in time

You have set my heart free, Us this perfect must be a crime

@letsgetlostbetweenthelines

©

you're why the book can't be shut

such déjà vu

Trust, that's just it

I've heard it all before

Words deep as a pit

Makes my heart sore

Just to think about

All that's took place

Do I need to reroute

To that very case

A flashback to the past

Just so you can see

How it feels to be last

How it feels to be me

Living with such Déjà vu

@letsgetlostbetweenthelines

©

you're why the book can't be shut

dream killer funder

You're the one word wonder
The dream killer funder
No reply for an hour
Makes my thoughts go sour
Are you really there
Do you just not care
Must be too busy
Oh what's her name this time
Trying to make me mad
It's all just sad
That you'd drop so low
But you reap what you sow
Remember that always

@letsgetlostbetweenthelines
©

you're why the book can't be shut

don't know

Don't know how I feel?

Then look into my eyes it shall be revealed

Don't know what I'm thinking?

Then open your ears you shall understand

Don't know what I'm saying?

Then listen to my words I am explaining

Don't know what I'm doing?

Then ask yourself where you went wrong

@letsgetlostbetweenthelines

©

you're why the book can't be shut

<u>endless buzzing</u>

Ever felt absolutely nothing, a complete silence

Just driving down the road and everything is a blur

Like you're driving really slow

But everything around you is in overdrive

Overwhelming

Just to think, nothing, a phone off the hook

Endless buzzing on the other end

Nobody there, but, you hold the phone

Human or not just waiting all the same

This feeling is like nothing else

It is tragedy all its own washing over you

Unexpectedly

Oceans that sneak up on you

Just as you're getting out, unexplainable emotions

Washing over you and swallows you whole

Claiming what is rightfully its, crashing over and over

Nowhere to run nowhere to hide

Just left to sit in silence to listen

To all the words pouring from your mouth

Dissociating

@letsgetlostbetweenthelines

©

you're why the book can't be shut

this I say

No matter what I do
You're a promise that I'll keep
This I say is true
Cause I surely fell in deep

@letsgetlostbetweenthelines
©

you're why the book can't be shut

passerby

And she wrote about him

Like an old 50s love story

Gone to war straight inside her heart

Returned only to find her gone

Wage of worlds apart

Both longing to be found near

Passing window shopper

Gazing within and without

No pleasantries exchanged

Just alive between the folds

@letsgetlostbetweenthelines

©

you're why the book can't be shut

liquid dreams

You, my muse, my inspiration
The embodiment of raw beauty and grace
I am in awe of the way you love
Fearlessly and without restraint

Your smile, a radiant beam of sunlight
Illuminating the darkest corners of my soul
Your touch, gentle as a summer breeze
Sending shivers down my spine like a soft tune

Your eyes, pools of liquid dreams
Where I dive into depths unknown
Your laughter, contagious as wildfire,
Setting my heart ablaze with every sound

@letsgetlostbetweenthelines
©

you're why the book can't be shut

<u>*she ticks for you*</u>

Listen to that clock

She ticks for you

Tick tick tick

Well-rounded weight

Slowly moves down

Being guided by singular chain

Twenty-four hours

She works for you

To keep you moving

Going through the motions

Around and round

Keeping you from being late

With each woohoo

Another hour has gone by

Listen to that clock

I tick for you

@letsgetlostbetweenthelines

©

you're why the book can't be shut

call me insane

Some call me crazy some call me insane

Either way I'm still racking your brain

Little do they know it's just part of the game

Living here like this is just too plain

Don't worry there is more to gain

Just open your heart and feel the rain

Don't be afraid to dance and forget all your pain

Like I said some feel the rain others just get wet

Which will you choose when thinking about me

@letsgetlostbetweenthelines

©

you're why the book can't be shut

<u>a life left reeling</u>

All the moments
All the laughter
All the late nights
All the happy ever after

They live at first meetings
They thrive in first touches
They surrender to the next times
But, the dreaded word haunts us

Alas, the unspoken left wanting
Tis, grief is retched for the living
Grieving it all one day at a time
A life left reeling inside my mind

Too much questioning did it happen
A lifetime ago the fish got away

@letsgetlostbetweenthelines

you're why the book can't be shut

<u>does fate intervene</u>

My thoughts of you consume me
Oh, how I pine for you, as days turn into nights
But love is fickle, as the seasons turn
You pull away, my soul begins to burn
Soon your words grow cold, like winters frost
What once was love, now seems forever lost
And wonder what would cause you to stray
Was I wrong, or fail to meet your sights

@letsgetlostbetweenthelines

you're why the book can't be shut

the decision you took

Friends from the start, Always talking up a storm

Then something tore us apart, My life now has a deform

We will see each other, I smile when you pass

But you seem to duck and cover, As I head to my class

I catch a glance from you, There you stand, alone

Still, you stand in the crowd, My eyes are stuck like glue

You start to raise your hand, Heart flutters for a wave

Instead, you grab your book, A new road I pave

Cause the decision you took, Leads me to believe

Of all the hints and games, That we will never be

The best friends we use to see

@letsgetlostbetweenthelines

©

you're why the book can't be shut

though you don't

Though you don't ask for advice, it is given

Though you don't ask to be picked up, you are carried

Though you don't ask to be loved, you are treasured

@letsgetlostbetweenthelines

©

you're why the book can't be shut

don't tell

Don't tell me you're too busy

When you're making time for other people

Don't tell me you can't talk

When you're blowing up other people's phones

Don't tell me you like me a lot

When you show me the least

Don't tell me I'm the one

When you're making me second best

Don't treat me like your bitch

When I just want to be your girl

Don't like what I have to say

Then you should've listened long ago

@letsgetlostbetweenthelines

©

you're why the book can't be shut

<u>one plus one</u>

God made you

Than made me

Put ours hands together

And whispered meant to be

Isn't that just so sweet

Those four lines, to be the end

One plus one equals two

Ah life, just on pretend

Oof, I said it there it's all out

Open to the half truths and lies

Creating a problem when there was none

We no longer need a disguise

@letsgetlostbetweenthelines

©

you're why the book can't be shut

fair warning

Such strong deliverance, Feelings growing so proliferous

With just one look, He will read you like a book

He is not messing around, A lose you are bound

Better watch out, Don't you dare pout

I gave you fair warning, Lest it disturbs your yearning

@letsgetlostbetweenthelines

©

you're why the book can't be shut

<u>*my body yearns*</u>

Every ounce of blood in my body yearns for you
Every drop of tears yearns for you
Every step by my feet yearns for you
Come hold me closer

Every second my eyes blink towards you
Every hour my thoughts follow you around
Every day my throat swallows you down
Come push me further

Every moment slipped us by too fast
Every chance not taken God only knows
Every missed date not being planned
Come ghost me faster.

@letsgetlostbetweenthelines
©

you're why the book can't be shut

<u>*night owl*</u>

He said, exactly

But what did he mean by it

Like night owl forever found him

Me staying up thinking over

Surely that keeps him up

Tale goes I dreamed a dream of you

Spoken into existence he sure did

One word response

Left me wanting

All I managed was stare at emptiness

No response from me

Gears turning all day

To what I could've said

Maybe I'll stay up longer tonight

Just to see how exactly works.

@letsgetlostbetweenthelines

©

you're why the book can't be shut

<u>*wrinkles of the cover*</u>

What if our lives began at the end

Life born into the wrinkles of the cover

A little extra care and need for a mend

Laying right next to your lover

What else would we need in that life

Everything we wanted already in our hands

You and me calling each other husband and wife

Each second more precious than hourglass sands

@letsgetlostbetweenthelines

©

you're why the book can't be shut

<u>*shadows*</u>

We're all afraid of what lies

beyond the darkness.

But it's the shadows that draws

us in closer.

@letsgetlostbetweenthelines

you're why the book can't be shut

self-checkout
Ever just want to checkout

Store shopping is no fun anymore

The cart is getting overfilled

Things that weren't even on the list

Everyone keeps asking for this and that

There too long among too much noise, SO MUCH NOISE

The bolts on the wheels you can hear turning

You've been spinning the plastic ring on the handle

Spinning it for seven aisles now over and over

Hoping that it'll become louder than the wheels

Louder than the kids and people

Louder than every item hitting the shelf to cart

You're finally at the checkout lanes

All the aisles are open and empty

That's what you're hoping

No one is open to help you, no one is calling you over

Self checkout is open where you have to do it yourself

If only you could self checkout and this wasn't a store

@letsgetlostbetweenthelines ©

*If there is ever a point where this is relatable. Please seek out help. There is help for you. Whether its depression, ppd, ptsd, abuse in any form, grief, substances, any kind of season. One day at a time.

you're why the book can't be shut

this content

It's an ocean outside, my kitty dreams inside
To be this content only a human dreams of such a ride
Curled up nose buried paws ready for dream mice
Deep sleep till morning riding the wind waves how nice

@letsgetlostbetweenthelines
©

you're why the book can't be shut

this shadow

It was then she realized the time

The time how it whisked away the fur

From his back down to his tail

Leaving patches of grey throughout and thin

His ear whisks gotten longer and whimsical

Grew more impatient with his food and treats

Couldn't keep it down but devoured every snack

His last meal could come any day so why not spoil

Naps grew longer into days he'd hide away

Find quiet solace beyond the warm winter rays

Outside adventures grew sparce for his paws weary

His purrs deeper and longer for comfort

The bed became just quite out of reach

It was then she realized twelve years had gone by

A warm fluffy kitty cat to follow her steps

Half her life she has depended on this shadow

@letsgetlostbetweenthelines

©

you're why the book can't be shut

the best doors

Dream of long days and quiet nights
A field of crops and flowers under starry lights
So fragrant so pure they fuel kiddos dreams
Land that some only read between the seams

Where slow food is grown by wild water
Rows you can skip and play with your father
Nurtured and processed by hands and toes
Using recipes a mother always knows

Slow food is the way God intended
Fast life is the way humans pretended
The best doors always open to a porch
Try not to burn it down with a torch

Plant that seed, God will do the rest, we're told

@letsgetlostbetweenthelines

©

you're why the book can't be shut

pretty please

Keep me alive through this time
Never give it away for a dime
A moment that we shared
Even when we were dared
To outlast our memories
Would you keep it pretty please

@letsgetlostbetweenthelines
©

you're why the book can't be shut

<u>still, quiet moments</u>

In retrospect, the hardships fade but the good times stay etched in the mind and heart in a way that can't be explained exactly.

How blessed are we to have such an abundance of "good times" to ponder over in the still, quiet moments.

Learning, excruciatingly slow sometimes, to connect to what is and let go of what we assume must be or could've been or should be.

If we know one truth at the core of our existence though, it's that God has lead us to this beautiful reality, and when we trust Him, our cup runneth over.

From here all we desire is to pour into other cups the love of our person that God has poured into our lives through the people and places that have intertwined themselves into their story and our own.

All anyone could ever hope for at the end we are welcomed with arms open and a good ole cheek pat.

@letsgetlostbetweenthelines

©

you're why the book can't be shut

whoever

You did it, I'm so proud of you.

Whoever you are out there.

And needed to read this.

It's another year of life.

Keep going, each day at a time.

@letsgetlostbetweenthelines

©

you're why the book can't be shut

Letter from Author:

Dear Readers and Wondering Souls,

May what you read here

Fill in the negative space

Drawing the emotions near

When you need another place

Sincerely,

Me

Thanks for reading!

Don't forget to sign up for the newsletter. Please add a review

on your desired social media or store platform you purchased

this book at.

Use Hashtags

#letsgetlostbetweenthelines

#yourewhythebookcantbeshut

Author Bio:

The author discovered her love for writing here and there in the chaos of adolescent youth. Has since adventured into motherhood family life where she escapes into a quiet Alaskan homestead and herbal business living. She thrives in knowledge beyond standard education, instead has her Master Gardener cert and is on track to obtain a Registered Herbalist title in the future. Most of all she surrounds herself with love of slow food, traditional living, and romanticizing whatever season appears into writing.

Podcast or Readings Inquiries:

If you would like to arrange podcast or readings, please reach out to the author through email which can be found in front of the book.

Read good and well. -xoxo